KONDI'S QUEST

Mysteries in Malawi, Book 1

Sylvia Stewart

Kondi's Quest
Mysteries in Malawi, Book 1

Cover design by Lynnette Bonner of Indie Cover Design –
www.indiecoverdesign.com

Cover Art by Tori Hastings

Scripture quotations are taken from The Holy Bible, New International Version®,
NIV®. Copyright © 1973, 1978, 1984 by Biblica, Inc.™ Used by permission. All
rights reserved worldwide.

ISBN: 1499691491
ISBN-13: 978-1499691498

Kondi's Quest is a work of fiction. References to real people, events,
establishments, organizations, or locales are intended only to provide a sense of
authenticity and are used fictitiously. All other characters, incidents, and dialogue
are drawn from the author's imagination.

DEDICATION

FOR MY GRANDCHILDREN:

Castle, Victoria, Caleb, Keera Jo, Tyrell, Clayton, Madison, Deryck, Isaac, Eliana, and Skye, who have captured my heart forever;

AND FOR THE CHILDREN OF AFRICA:

who always tugged at my heart strings.

ACKNOWLEDGMENTS

In memoriam, I am deeply grateful to my parents, Lionel and Eltha Furman, who loved me unconditionally and believed I could accomplish any project.

To my brother, Jim Furman, thank you for loving me and believing in me.

I also thank my dear husband, Duane, who has supported and financed my writing endeavors. Grateful hugs, honey.

Special thanks to Tori Hastings, my dear granddaughter, of whom I'm so proud. She drew the cover art.

Deep gratitude is also due to Marjorie Stewart, my writing instructor, mentor and friend. Donna Fleisher gave me an in-depth critique of this novel and encouraged me to finish it. My daughter, Lynnette Bonner, and other dear friends, Tammy Perron, Barbara Lighthizer and Cris Ortmann, gave me invaluable help and encouragement. Thank you so much.

CHAPTER 1

I wonder if Bambo would give me fifty tambala for thread. Chikondi carried a tin cup of steaming, sweet tea. Very carefully she shifted the hot cup from one hand to the other, but she kept her eyes on the silver rim where the tea might slosh over. She was afraid to ask him. She couldn't tell him it was for embroidery thread. He'd be so angry! She knew there were no extra tambala for what he would call "nonsense." She glanced up at him. He sat on the far side of their earthen yard, the unbuttoned sleeves of his red-and-black-checked shirt pushed up his arms.

She looked at the tea leaves moving in the bottom of the cup, patterns swimming and changing. In her mind she saw the design she was sewing. *If only I had some more red thread to finish it. Maybe after he's had his tea, I can ask him. But he's been looking at the papers in his brown envelope again, and then he's always cross.*

The tea was light and clear because her mother had put lemon in it instead of milk. Last night

Bambo had taken his brown envelope and gone to the bar to drink. He was there until late in the night. He preferred lemon in his morning tea after he had been drinking.

Now he sat in the deep shade of an avocado tree at the edge of the clearing around their house. Near him the big brown envelope rested across some stones to keep it from getting dirty.

Kondi shifted the cup in her hands again, being very careful not to spill it as she walked across the yard. *He'll go to sleep after his tea,* she thought. *I'd better ask him when he wakes up.*

Bending to hand the cup to Bambo, she tripped on a stick of firewood in front of her foot. With the next step she stumbled. Hot tea spilled over her hand. She jerked, and scalding tea poured down her father's arm to his elbow and onto the brown envelope below.

"Ahh!" Bambo yelled, shaking his scalded arm. "Worthless child! You are always careless!"

Kondi's hand flew to her mouth. "Mai-o! Pepani! Don't beat—" Bambo's fist slashed toward Kondi's head. She threw up her arm to protect herself. Bambo's hand connected and she spun sideways across the hard-packed yard. As she fell in the gravel on one knee, a chicken flapped away with a loud squawk.

"My envelope! You've ruined my envelope!" Bambo danced with rage.

Needles of pain stabbed through her head. Clutching her ear and clamping her eyes shut she clenched her teeth to keep from crying. Jumping to her feet, she stumbled down the short path to the road, opening her eyes long enough to drop over the steep embankment onto the dirt roadside.

A truck loaded with bags of maize careened around the corner. Fear squeezed Kondi's heart and pumped her feet into a wild dash. She leaped up the bank on the other side of the road and grabbed a handful of coarse grass with one hand, thrashing like a rabbit in a snare. The truck blared as it roared behind her. With the other hand she caught the root of a tree and hauled herself up. Men sat laughing on the top of the bags of maize. Throwing herself into the rough grass, Kondi wriggled from bush to bush, crawling on her hands and knees. After a bit she stopped to rest beneath a flame tree.

"Where are you? I'll beat you flat!"

Kondi's head jerked around.

"You've ruined my envelope! I'll beat your skinny bones!" Her father stood on the road bank brandishing a stout stick over his head. She scrambled away through the weeds deeper into the brush.

Finally, exhausted, she propped herself under the shade of a large protea bush with its spiky pink-and-white flowers turning themselves inside out. Tears began to roll down her cheeks as she rubbed her stinging face and aching ear. *The meaning of my name is a cruel joke.* A trickle of blood ran down her leg. *Love. Hah To me, love is only a dream. Mai may love me, but Bambo doesn't. If only he would!*

"I hate Bambo!" she asserted angrily, plucking a soft leaf to wipe away the blood. She remembered the laughing men in the truck. "I hate them, too!" In her mind she threw rocks at them.

After a while she heard her mother calling from the edge of the road, but she didn't answer.

Kondi moaned to herself. *No one loves me – not even Mai. Why does Bambo beat me? I didn't mean to spill the tea. Even adults have accidents sometimes.* Kondi held one hand to her throbbing ear. She knew Mai would never leave Bambo, but she wished, somehow, for their home to be a place of peace, instead of fear. Using another leaf, she wiped her knee again—red blood on warm brown skin.

When the sun beamed high overhead, she stood up and started down the hill toward the well near the bottom where she could wash her knee and get a drink. She gazed at the purple-blue mountains across the wide valley. They seemed painted against the blue sky, so clear she felt she could reach out and touch them. Each peak wore a fluffy white cloud. *Like old, humped women with wooly hats on.* But seeing the purple mountains like that didn't make her feel happy as it usually did.

At the well, Kondi put her leg under the spout. The hot metal handle reminded her of the hot tin tea cup and all the morning's trouble. The pump screeched several times before warm water gushed over her leg. Gingerly, she washed the dried blood from her knee and gently blotted it with the hem of her skirt.

Just then she heard steps on the path. Someone was coming! *Is that Bambo's red and black shirt?* Fear pulsed into her fingertips as she started to run.

"Kondi."

She stopped and turned. It was her mother. Kondi stood still near a bush, punching holes in one of its broad leaves with her fingernail. She looked at her mother, and then looked away.

"I've been calling and calling you, Kondi."

"I didn't burn him on purpose, Mai. I didn't! It was an accident."

"Of course it was." Mai moved closer. "I wasn't calling you to punish you. Are you all right? Your knee is bleeding!" She began to pump a bucket full to the brim while she talked. "Come. I'll send you to the clinic in town. You need a bandage. On your way home you can stop at the market to buy greens for supper."

Most of the girls her age had several brothers and sisters to look after. "Maybe Mai will have a baby girl soon," she would tell her friends at school. "Then I'll have a baby sister to carry on my back, just like the rest of you!"

Today, though, on her long walk to town, she felt too worried to even think about having a baby sister. She kept seeing her father's fist come slashing down toward her head. Usually she enjoyed the scorching sun on her shoulders and seeing the wild flowers and butterflies. Usually she would stop near the road and take a long look at the black tracery of the jacaranda tree, with its lavender breath of blossom. Usually she would skip and run and call to her friends.

Today she walked head down, shoulders drooped, whacking here and there with a stick, raising dust. She struck at a yellow butterfly. It fell to the road and thrashed away with a torn wing. Kondi turned and walked backward, watching the butterfly stagger and dip in its erratic flight.

What's in Bambo's envelope anyway? Kondi dragged her stick in the dust. *He carries it everywhere. Is there money in there, or letters, or what?* She sighed heavily. *I can't see how an old torn envelope can be so important.*

Suddenly, she bumped into something warm and soft. *Bambo!* She squinched her eyes and threw her hands up to protect her head. Something fell with a thud and a rattle, like spilling gravel. Metallic prickles of fear danced across her tongue.

CHAPTER 2

When the blow didn't come, Kondi cautiously opened one eye. Ulemu Mbewe, her best friend, stood in front of her with her hands on her hips.

"Hello, Kondi. You should watch where you're going instead of where you've been!" Ulemu's voice was reproachful, but her eyes began to crinkle at the corners. A basket of maize lay in the road with a white heap of maize kernels spilling out onto the dirt.

"Sorry." Kondi stooped down. "I'll help you pick it up."

As both girls bent to scoop up the maize, they heard a snicker behind them. "Too bad you spilt the maize. Have fun picking it up!" Boniko, the meanest girl in the village, stuck out her tongue and made a face as she walked on by.

"Boniko could have helped us." Kondi sighed as they put the last of the maize back in the basket. She helped Ulemu lift the basket back on her head.

"I'm going to the chigayo. Where are you going?"

Ulemu asked.

"To the clinic in town." Kondi lifted the hem of her skirt to show her injured knee. "Then I'll stop at the market to buy cabbage for supper."

They started walking purposefully toward the maize mill and town.

"How'd you cut your knee?"

"When Bambo hit me I fell down. He's been drinking again. I was carrying tea to him and accidentally spilled it on his arm." Kondi gulped a deep breath. "Worse than that, I spilled it on his brown envelope, but I didn't do it on purpose."

"Of course you didn't." Ulemu smiled. "What's in his envelope anyway? We see him carrying it all the time and our whole family wonders about it."

"I don't know. Whatever it is, it must be very valuable, because he locks it in his drawer at night. And when he looks at the papers in it, he always goes off by himself and turns his back, so we never can see."

"It would be fun to peek," Ulemu said with a twinkle in her eye.

"Don't you dare even think about it. I'd be blamed and he'd beat me again."

Suddenly Ulemu screamed. "Pinching ants!" She clutched the basket to her head and ran up the road. "They are all over me!"

Kondi looked at the road and there was a black trail of ants starting to scatter in the center where they had stepped. Kondi's neck tingled with goose bumps. "Eee! me, too!" Tickling ants crawled up her legs and around her waist. "Mai-o! They're pinching me all over!" She screamed and grabbed first her neck and then the back of her leg.

Both girls dashed behind some bushes and flung off their clothes to pick off the ants as fast as they could. "Ow! Another one on my shoulder!" Kondi giggled hysterically watching Ulemu twist on one foot trying to reach her back. "Let me help you," she said, reaching for the black spot on Ulemu's shoulder blade.

Kondi slapped her knee, howling with laughter. "You're dancing like old Gogo Mwale when she's had too much to drink!" She swatted at her own ear, flinging another ant into the bushes. Both girls laughed until they fell over into the grass.

When they had picked off all the pinching ants they carefully checked their clothes and dressed again. Then they sat down for a short rest.

"My mother says sins are like pinching ants," Ulemu said. "They never come alone." Ulemu checked her leg to see if an itchy place was another ant. "If you steal sugar from the kitchen cupboard, you have to be deceitful and lie to cover it up as well."

Kondi imagined a long, winding trail of sins twisting away behind her into the distance. "That's true," she murmured. "One lie makes you tell another one to cover it up." She rubbed a hand over her black curly hair.

They stood and she helped Ulemu lift the basket to her head again. Puffs of red dust powdered their bare feet as they walked on.

"It's too bad your father drinks all the time," Ulemu said. "He didn't used to drink, did he?"

"Not until he lost his job. But now he drinks a lot." Kondi brushed a fly from her arm and plucked on a grass stem to chew. "I guess God can't be a loving God, like the Bible says He is, or He wouldn't let Bambo beat me like this. I go to church all the time, and I try to live like the Bible says. Is this my reward?" She lifted the hem of her skirt and examined her knee. She frowned and covered her aching ear with her hand.

"Does your ear ache, too?" Ulemu asked.

Kondi nodded. "He hit my head and I fell."

"I'm sorry." Ulemu's face looked sober.

Kondi bit her lower lip. "He beats Mai sometimes, and she's going to have a baby. The old ladies in the village say babies are found near the well when the women go for water, but I know where babies come from." Kondi's voice choked up. "If he beats her again, the baby could die and I want a baby sister so much!"

Ulemu seemed at a loss for words. "I'm sorry, Kondi. But the Bible is true and God is good. We'll pray about this. You'll see. God will turn it into good, I just know it."

"I've prayed and prayed, and I don't see any help from God," Kondi replied.

"Maybe He'll hear you and your mother, since you're such good Christians." Ulemu's mother taught their Sunday school class.

Ulemu swallowed hard. "Well, you don't have to be a 'good Christian' for God to hear your prayers. He hears all of His children when they pray."

"Well, He doesn't hear my prayers."

"Oh yes He does," Ulemu said. "Don't you remember the Bible story Mai taught us in Sunday school where the prince of Persia stopped the angel of God who was bringing God's answer to Daniel's prayer? God had heard and sent an answer, but Satan prevented the angel from bringing the answer quickly. He hears all our prayers, but the devil is at work in the world, too, Kondi."

"Yes, I remember. I guess I'm just tired of being hit. Please don't stop praying for me, Ulemu."

"Let's pray now." The two girls stopped in the shade of a tree beside the road and closed their eyes. "God, please help Kondi to remember that you do answer prayer. And whatever is troubling her father, I pray that you will show him that he needs to ask You for help. We pray it in Jesus' name, amen."

"Thank you for praying and being such a good friend." Kondi smiled shyly at Ulemu.

"Well, here's where I stop," Ulemu said, when they came to the chigayo a few minutes later. "Come see me this afternoon when you get back from Dedza. Remember, Kondi, I'm praying for you."

"Thanks." Kondi ducked under the basket on

Ulemu's head so she could give her a hug.

Ulemu turned off the road onto the path to the chigayo. They smiled at each other as they parted. Kondi turned, walking backward to call goodbye to Ulemu.

Back the road a ways, a woman sat in the shade of a tree. A pot of beer, covered with a banana leaf, sat on the ground beside her—and there was Bambo, handing money to the woman! As Kondi watched, he drank down a whole gourdful of beer, and then wiped his mouth on his red-and-black-checked sleeve. He turned to stagger down the road in their direction, his big brown envelope clutched under his arm.

Fear nearly choked her. "Ulemu, he's following me!" Kondi ran up the chigayo path and clutched her friend's arm. "He hasn't seen me yet. Quick!" They dashed up the path past the chigayo house and crouched down behind a clump of banana trees.

"Please, God, don't let Bambo find me!" Kondi whispered this simple prayer over and over.

CHAPTER 3

Kondi peeked around the corner of the chigayo building. Her heart throbbed in her throat.

Out on the road Bambo stumbled, veering across the road in a diagonal stagger. He lifted his brown envelope high over his head and mumbled a drunken tune. Apparently, he didn't see her. He tottered on down the dusty road past the mill.

Kondi sighed and rested her head against the gritty dried mud of the building's wall. She sat there for a long time, still, staring at the ground. Neither Kondi nor Ulemu said a word. Finally, Kondi whispered, "I don't think I will meet him anywhere on the road. I'll have to keep watch for him in town."

In town at the clinic Kondi approached the door and peered cautiously around the door jamb. Walls glared white in the early afternoon sun streaming through the windows. As she slipped through the door, and approached the nurse's station she wrinkled her nose. The room smelled of medicine and strong soap.

She sat on the long bench by the door and twisted and turned while she waited. *I wish I was back home. At least Bambo didn't find me, so God must have heard my prayer.* A thin smile turned up the corners of her mouth.

"Kondi Chisale?" the nurse asked.

Kondi's heart bumped against her ribs as she followed the nurse's white back.

"Sit there," the nurse said in a cross voice.

Kondi watched with round eyes as the nurse laid out a gauze pad, iodine, and tape. Her leg jerked and she winced when the nurse dabbed iodine on the cut, but she didn't make a sound. Then the nurse wrapped a bandage around her knee and tied it snugly.

Before she went out of the clinic, she peeked around the door jamb to make sure Bambo was nowhere outside. When she walked into the sun, it dazzled her eyes and the bandage made her limp as she walked toward the market.

I hate town! She wove her way between the crowds at the entrance to the market. *Everyone seems unfriendly, and there is so much noise.* She walked up behind a woman who stopped to show her tax card to the gate guard. She pretended to be the woman's daughter, but quickly slipped away once they were inside the gate. *I hope the gatekeeper didn't notice me leave her and realize I didn't show a tax card. He's a cross old man.*

A vendor fried pieces of meat on a charcoal brazier just inside the market gate. Her gaze paused on the smoking meat strips and she licked her lips, but she didn't stop. She hurried past the women who sold maize meal by the plateful from huge granite bowls heaped high with cones of white flour. She stepped over strips of bicycle inner-tubes and the hand-woven rope that people used to tie things on the backs of their bicycles.

Skirting the corner of a stand holding used bicycle parts, she nearly ran into a man bent double under a load of dried fish that he had brought to sell. Vendors squatted by piles of used clothing. She covered her ears with her hands as she walked by the tin smiths who made a deafening noise as they pounded their tin into cups, pans, buckets, and dippers.

Smiling, she finally stepped into the shade of the cool open shed where the cabbages, potatoes, tomatoes, oranges, bananas, and peanuts were heaped close together on gunny sacks. Reaching for a cabbage, she knocked over a pile of oranges.

"You!" shouted the old woman who sold them. Kondi threw her hand up to her face, expecting a blow. "Be careful!" The old woman scowled, her forehead furrowed into a frown.

"Pepani," Kondi whispered.

After she paid for the cabbage, there were two coins left. *I'd like to buy red thread for my sewing. Mai*

said *I could spend the change on something I want.*
She walked slowly to a rickety stand near the gate
offering soap, thread, rice, needles, Cokes, and
candy.

For a long time her eyes darted between the red
thread and the candies in a jar. *I wish I could tell
Bambo and Mai that I like to draw designs on cloth
and embroider them, but I'm afraid they would laugh.*
She remembered how the villagers had laughed
when Bambo planted flowers by their front door.
"You're just making your house beautiful so ours will
look bad," they said.

Would her friends say things like that if she made
her dresses pretty? *When Baby Sister comes, I'll
embroider beautiful designs on all her dresses.* Kondi
smiled. *I won't care if the whole village laughs.*

She looked longingly at the bright skeins of thread
lying in small boxes. *I think I'll buy the sweets instead;
one for Mai because I love her, and one for Bambo so
maybe he will begin to love me, too.*

"Aha!" A sinewy hand clamped her shoulder.
Kondi whirled around and started to run, thinking it
was Bambo.

Boniko grinned at her, flouncing her skirt in
delight at her mean joke. "Hello, Kondi!" Boniko's
voice had an impish tone. "Let's walk home
together."

I don't really want to walk home with her. She
swallowed hard and gave two tambala to the man
behind the counter. She pointed to the candy; her
throat was too dry to speak. *But I can't refuse; it*

wouldn't be polite. She tucked the two candies in the pocket of her petticoat, wrapped her chirundu snuggly around her waist and turned reluctantly toward the gate.

"What happened to your knee?" Boniko asked as they started up the road.

"I cut it, of course."

"Of course!" Boniko grinned, but she didn't say anything more.

The girls chattered about school and friends. At the edge of town they picked scarlet hibiscus flowers and pushed the stems into the curly black hair above their ears. Kondi heaved a sigh when they reached the country road. Now she could hear the birds sing and the sigh of the wind in the elephant grass. Angular cranes cawed to each other in a top-heavy tree by the road, their call as metallic as gravel swirled in a bucket.

Near the grain mill, Kondi looked for Ulemu, but, apparently, she had already left, carrying the heavy basket, heaped high with maize flour on her head.

Their shadows stretched long on the ground. When they came to the pinching ant tree. Kondi walked carefully. "Ulemu and I got into pinching ants here this morning," she told Boniko. "Eee, we had much trouble. They pinched us all over!"

"They only pinch—you won't die," Boniko scoffed.

"I know, but I don't like them." Kondi shivered. The ants had gone—there was only a narrow mark in the dust left by their millions of tiny feet. It looked as if someone had dragged a head of grass across the road. Kondi put her finger in the mark. "You go on, Boniko I want to sit here and think for a while." She looked at the ground and scuffed her toe in the dust.

"Well, don't cut your knee again, squatting there." Boniko laughed. "And watch out for pinching ants." She wrinkled her nose and stuck out her tongue at Kondi as she walked away.

Kondi relaxed as she looked out over the wide valley in the late afternoon light. From here she could see white clouds heaped up behind the purple mountains and spilling through the passes. The lowering sun rimmed each cloud top with gold.

As soon as Boniko disappeared around the bend in the road, Kondi sat down under the pinching ant tree and squeezed her eyes shut. Her mouth didn't move, but she talked to God. *Do You see me sitting here? My knee is sore, but I'm kneeling in my heart. Because You can see everywhere, You know my heart is filled with sin, one following the other, like the pinching ants. I've been bad, but I want to be good. I've hated Bambo, but I know You want me to love him. Please be my friend and take hatred out of my heart. I want to love Bambo, and I want him to love You – and me, too. And please help Baby Sister to come safely.*

She took the hibiscus flower out of her hair and found a crack in the bark of the tree. She pushed the stem of the scarlet flower into it. *This marks the place where I talked with God. I'll remember this day every time I pass this tree. The flower will fade, but I'll never forget."*

Before she stepped back into the road, she looked

back toward town. In the late afternoon light the road wound away like a reddish-brown ribbon weaving in and out of the low hills. Back and back...she could see almost to the crossroads. Suddenly her heart stopped. Down the road she could see someone coming—someone in a red-and-black-checked shirt. The figure waved its arms and lurched from one side of the road to the other. Kondi took a deep breath, swallowed hard and hurried home.

CHAPTER 4

The next Sunday Boniko scooted down the bench toward Kondi in Sunday school class. "Here we are to listen to Ugly Teacher again." She giggled in Kondi's ear. "Look at the mole on her chin."

"You mustn't say Teacher is ugly," Kondi whispered. "It isn't kind." She didn't want to laugh, but she felt her eyes begin to crinkle at the corners. "Besides, Ulemu's mother is too nice to be ugly."

"I don't feel like being kind today. Watch this." Esinati and Losi sat on the bench in front of them. Boniko reached up and pinched the soft skin on the back of Losi's neck. Losi shrieked, and the whole class turned around to look. Boniko scooted down the bench, pushing Kondi in front of her until Kondi fell off the end.

"Girls!" scolded Mai Mbewe. "Let's be quiet so we can begin our lesson."

Kondi pushed up from the floor and pulled her extra chirundu up over her face. Her heart was pounding and she tried to stop her nervous giggling.

Boniko made a loud snort that started the whole class tittering and shifting in their seats.

"Quiet please!" Mai Mbewe said. "We have a very interesting lesson today."

Boniko wasn't listening. She was busy picking up a large ant carefully...carefully so as not to squash it.

"No!" Kondi whispered.

But Boniko raised her hand high and dropped it on Esinati's head. It began to crawl slowly over her curly hair, closer and closer to Esinati's ear. Boniko nudged Kondi and pointed to the ant. Closer and closer! Suddenly Esinati jumped and swatted at her ear. She shook her head again and again. Kondi and Boniko clapped their hands over their mouths, but the giggles slipped through their fingers in bubbles and squeaks. Everyone began laughing again.

Mai Mbewe stopped talking. She walked back to their bench, took Boniko's hand, and sat her on the front row. Mai Mbewe faced the class. "Kondi, have you ever been afraid?"

Kondi felt little cold bumps begin to rise on the back of her neck. "Afraid?" She tried to look brave, but her voice sounded strange even to herself. *I'm always afraid of Bambo! If I knew Bambo loved me, it would help me to not be afraid of so many things.*

Then she remembered last night. She had been kept later than usual at the grain mill. The sun was going down when she raised the basket of flour onto her head and started for home. By the time she got near the graveyard, it was dark. Walking faster, Kondi glanced at the graveyard and then back to the road. "Don't fall. Something might be in there," she whispered to herself. She opened her eyes wide and peered into the shadows.

Suddenly, the bushes rustled! Fear ran down into Kondi's fingers like cold water. She gripped the basket on her head and began to run. The Thing found the road and ran after her. She ran faster. The Thing panted behind her. Faster! Faster! A light shone from the fire in Mai Phiri's cook-house. Running toward it, Kondi burst through the doorway, nearly knocking Mai Phiri into her own cooking fire. She flattened her back against the far wall, holding the basket of flour on her head with both hands. Her breath came in short, quick gasps.

"What's the matter, Kondi?" Mai Phiri shouted, righting herself in front of the fire. "Be careful! You're about to knock the porridge pot over!"

"Look!" Kondi pointed a shaking finger at the eyes glowing in the doorway. "Something is chasing me from the graveyard!" The Thing took a step into the light. Ukhale, her father's dog, stood in the doorway, with his tongue hanging out the side of his mouth. Kondi's breath came in a long sigh.

"Yes, it is your own dog," Mai Phiri said. "You come running in here to get away from your own dog?"

"I thought it was...it came out of the graveyard...I was afraid."

"Go home! Get out of my kitchen and take your dog with you!" Mai Phiri waved a winnowing basket at her to shoo her out the door. "The next time you are afraid of something in the graveyard..."

But Kondi didn't wait to hear the rest of what Mai Phiri had to say. She scurried away for home with Mai Phiri's voice fading away behind her.

"Kondi!"

Yesterday's memory faded like morning mist in the sunshine.

Mai Mbewe was looking at her, waiting for an answer. "I asked if you have ever been afraid."

"Yes," Kondi whispered. Her heart pounded even now. She licked her lips and rubbed at the goose-bumps on the back of her neck.

"Today's Bible story is about some men who were afraid," Mai Mbewe said. "One day at twilight when the first evening star appeared, Jesus and His disciples got in a boat to cross a lake. They hadn't been rowing long when a strong wind began to blow. The boat was still far from the shore. The wind whipped up big waves sloshing, sloshing." Mai Mbewe's arm wagged back and forth. "Water began to pour over the side and fill the boat! They dipped the water out as fast as they could, but waves kept splashing in. 'What will we do?' the men asked each other. 'Soon we will drown!'"

"Why didn't they jump into the lake and swim?" Boniko asked. "It is silly to stay in a boat that is going to sink."

"That's true," Mai Mbewe replied, "but the waves were so big the men couldn't swim. 'Let's ask Jesus what to do,' they said to each other. 'He's asleep in the back of the boat.'"

"Asleep?" Losi's hand shot up. "How could He be asleep in such a great storm? The men were shouting and clanking buckets and things weren't they?"

"Jesus wasn't afraid," Mai Mbewe said. "You can sleep when you are not afraid."

Kondi listened with both ears now. *I'm always afraid. Before I was only afraid of Bambo. Now I'm afraid of many things: hooting trucks, things in the graveyard, and being alone in the dark. What can I do? My baby sister will need me to be brave, not afraid all the time.*

Just then a huge cypress cone fell from the tree outside onto the metal roof of their classroom. Kondi jumped, and then glanced around at the others. No one else seemed to have noticed.

It's Bambo's fault! If Bambo loved me, he'd stop hitting me, and I would stop being afraid of everything. She swallowed the lump in her throat to keep from crying.

Mai Mbewe's voice went on with the story, but Kondi didn't hear. Again, she remembered a few days before when some boys at school found a chameleon and carried it around on a stick to scare all the girls. Kondi was playing dodge ball. She hadn't seen them coming. Suddenly, the ugly lizard was right in front of her face. Its fat fleshy tongue rolled around in its toothy, gaping mouth. It hissed at her. One of its eyes rolled back and its tail began to uncurl. Even now Kondi's heart pounded. She wanted to lick her lips, but her tongue stuck to the roof of her mouth. *What can I do so I'll stop being afraid?*

"The Bible says that 'Perfect love casts out fear'," Mai Mbewe's voice said, interrupting Kondi's thoughts. "When we love God and really trust Him, then we don't have to be afraid any more. We can trust Him to be our protector and friend."

Kondi nodded. *I need a protector and friend.*

"'Trust in the Lord with all your heart,' the Bible says." Mai Mbewe continued the lesson. "When we ask God to be our friend, we can trust Him always to be with us and help us when we are afraid."

She remembered the pinching ant tree and her talk with God. *I don't have to be afraid any more. I just need to trust God. He will protect me.*

CHAPTER 5

On Monday evening Kondi dreaded to have her father come home. Any moment she expected to hear his voice singing drunkenly at the turning of the road, or the thud of his lurching steps in the hard-packed yard, but he did not come. Mai waited with supper for about an hour, because Bambo always ate first. Finally, she and Kondi ate and washed their dishes.

Kondi, tired from helping her mother all day, rolled out her sleeping mat in a corner of the bedroom, wrapped herself in her blanket, and lay down. Her thoughts returned to that morning.

Bambo had been digging along the path from the road to their house. He had some flower cuttings that he intended to plant on either side. Boniko's father came along the road just as Bambo was beginning to put in the first cutting.

"Moni, Chisale. How are you?" Boniko's father asked. "I see you are going to plant flowers. Flowers are for women and old folks. Are you trying to make your house look better than the rest of ours?"

Bambo forced a smile, but his eyes were dark with suppressed anger. As soon as Boniko's father walked out of sight, Bambo threw the rest of the cuttings on the garbage heap and walked away, muttering, toward the local bar.

Outside in the moonlight, a cricket scraped his fiddle at the corner of the house. *Why are people like that?* Kondi yawned deeply. *Last month our other neighbor made fun of Bambo for cutting the ragged grass on the eaves of our thatched roof. It made Bambo angry, but he finished all the way around the house. I like pretty things. They make me happy.* A chicken ruffled its feathers and croaked in the little round chicken house on the other side of the open window. Kondi's eyes felt heavy with sleep, but she stared at the gyrations of three mosquitoes dancing in a shaft of moonlight. Their tiny shadows danced in the white square of moonlight on the floor. Finally, she folded her arm under her head for a pillow and pulled the blanket up over her head to protect herself from mosquitoes. Soon she was asleep.

A loud shout woke her. Kondi flung back her blanket and sat straight up on her mat. The white square on the floor was gone. Someone shouted and a bucket clanked loudly in the dark. Bambo's slurred voice demanded his supper.

Mai said, "I have food for you. It will only take a minute to heat it." A chair creaked as her mother stood heavily to her feet to reheat the food.

"I don't want to wait. I want to eat now!" Bambo

roared with rage, and the bucket crashed and clattered into the yard. His drunken muttering broke into another snarl. A chair cracked as it hit the wall. The table crashed over. Kondi huddled as far into her corner as she could, turned her face away and hid her eyes.

Kondi heard a resounding slap. She winced and ducked her head.

A thud. Mai moaned as she fell against the wall.

Kondi crawled along the wall, hid in the farthest corner of the bedroom and plugged her ears. Still she could hear as the beating went on and on. Blood pulsed in her throat. In her mind she screamed, *Don't hit Mai! Don't hit Mai!* But no sound came. Hot tears spilled down her cheeks. Her chest ached from her own pounding heart, and searing hot breaths dried her mouth. Fear prickled across her scalp and blood drummed in her temples.

The beating stopped as suddenly as it had begun. A body fell against the table and then to the floor. Bambo muttered and cursed. He crashed into the wall, fumbled for the door and staggered out into the night.

The complete silence frightened Kondi as much as the noise. "Mai!"

No answer.

"Mai!" she said louder.

Silence.

Kondi crept to the doorway of the sitting room. Mai lay on the floor with her hand on her stomach. Blood trickled from a corner of her mouth.

She's dead! Mai and my baby sister are dead! Father has killed them both! She leaped to her feet and ran out the door screaming, "Mai-o! Mai-o! My mother is dead!"

The yard suddenly churned with neighbors, their eyes wide with alarm. Kondi staggered to the shadow of the maize garner and fell to the ground, sobbing. With Mai gone, who would take care of her? Only her drunken father! Fear snatched at her and her body jerked and trembled. People hurried here and there helping Mai, but Kondi only rocked herself in the moon-shadow of the maize crib, moaning over and over, "Mai-o! Mai-o! Mai-o!"

"Kondi?" A hand shook her shoulder. Mai Mbewe's voice sounded close to her ear. "Your mother is not dead, only badly hurt. You must come in the ox cart with us to take her to the hospital. She needs you, Kondi. Come!"

The oxen bawled their midnight displeasure. Mai's groans of pain punctuated the night as the ox cart lurched over the rough road. Mai Mbewe bent over her as the cart rumbled on, wiping her face with a cold wet cloth. Kondi wiped her own face with the corner of her chirundu, her sobs making a breath-cloud in the chilly night air. Her heart ached during the whole, long, moonlit journey.

At the hospital, she stepped out of the cart and into a shadowed corner. Nurses put Mai on a bed with wheels and pushed her through a yellow-lighted doorway. Kondi sat on the cold damp ground with her back against the wall. Mai Mbewe sat down beside her.

"Mai isn't dead yet, but she may die soon!" Kondi sobbed. "She may die soon, and my baby sister, too!" After a while she realized she was alone again. Mai Mbewe must have gone to be with her mother.

Hours later Mai Mbewe found her there with her chirundu over her head, shivering in half-sleep, as the dawn etched the eastern hills with a gold and crimson line. "Come, Kondi," Mai Mbewe said. "Your mother is asking for you." Her voice sounded tired and, taking Kondi's hand, she led her into the hospital.

Kondi hung back and glanced around in fright. She had heard many times that a hospital was a place to go to die. She almost expected to see the face of Death leering at her from around a corner, or behind a door. Mai lay on a bed near the door of her room. Her eyes were closed and a nurse held her wrist. The bandage circling her head showed starkly white against her smooth brown skin. Under the edge of the bandage an ugly bruise formed and blood seeped through to the surface. Kondi stopped short. "Will she die?" she whispered.

"Iai," the nurse said with a smile. Her crisp, white uniform rustled, and she smelled of sweet soap. "No, a hospital is a place to get well. We will help her all we can." She smiled and beckoned Kondi to come near.

Mai opened her eyes and slowly turned her head. A weak smile softened her mouth, but she winced when she tried to lift her arm.

"I'm sorry, Mai," Kondi whispered. "I was too afraid to do anything."

"You couldn't do anything," Mai said softly, rubbing Kondi's arm with her good hand. "But you can do something now. This hospital doesn't supply food. I will need good food to make me well. Mai Mbewe will give you money to go buy a chicken at the market. Will you do that for me? Be sure it is a fat one." Mai always said that when she sent Kondi for a chicken.

Kondi felt better hearing her talk in her usual way. "Yes, I'll buy a fat one, Mai." Tears blurred her eyes as she walked out to the hospital garden. She paced restlessly, shivering in the cold morning air. *What is taking Mai Mbewe so long?*

Soon the sun topped the eastern hills and bathed the yard with warm yellow light. Kondi backed up against the sunlit wall, and wrapped her extra chirundu closer around her shoulders. The sun felt good and her shivering lessened.

At the edge of the yard three peach trees huddled together as if for company. Their froth of pink blossoms lightly perfumed the air. Kondi closed her eyes and turned her face to the sun to enjoy the fragrance of the flowers and the sun's warmth. *I'll embroider pink flowers like those on one of my baby sister's dresses.* A tiny smile lifted the corners of her mouth. *She'll soon be here.*

Suddenly the inside of her eyelids went dark. Her eyes flew open in alarm. A dark cloud had swallowed the sun, and an icy wind whipped down from the purple mountains, driving dust wraiths along the ground. Kondi hunched her shoulders as her chirundu whipped her ankles.

The peach trees bent in the wind, their branches dipping and thrashing. Kondi squatted by the hospital wall and covered her head with her extra chirundu. Inside her chirundu tent she listened to the gusts that skittered leaves over the ground. She made a peephole to look out. A piece of newspaper scraped past her feet and plastered itself against the hospital fence.

The peach trees writhed as if in pain, their delicate blossoms turning inside out, then back. A few petals twisted away on the wind, then more. Soon pink petals danced all over the yard, stripped from their branches, streaming away in twisting trails. Kondi's heart thumped in fear. "Is this an omen of death? Does this mean my baby sister will die?" She swallowed hard. "Maybe Mai, too!"

The cold, whipping wind flung her words out over the Rift Valley far below.

CHAPTER 6

Several minutes later, heart still heavy, Kondi tied the five-kwacha bill Mai Mbewe gave her into the corner of her chirundu, pulled the cloth tightly around her waist and tucked in the corner to hold it in place. It was much too early for the market to be open, but she could wait at the bus stop near the market gate. It would be better to watch the travelers come and go than to sit by the wall of the hospital, thinking.

Quickly, she walked down the narrow path that led to the road. The wind snatched at her clothes. She picked a wild flower and plucked the orange petals, dropping them, and watching them stream away on the wind. "I won't think," she whispered to herself. "I won't think. I'll just watch the people and the buses."

At the bus stop everyone hurried. A bus arrived and the flock of pigeons that lived near the market flew up in a fluttering mass to the top of the bus, pecking at a passenger's sacks of maize tied onto the luggage rack. Conductors called for passengers. Travelers rushed to grab their bundles, and vendors shouted the praises of their wares. "Ripe bananas! Peanuts!" Arms reached out of the bus windows to buy roasted maize or a mango.

Kondi found a place close to the inside wall of the bus shelter. She didn't want to think, but thoughts came anyway. Scenes from all the sad events that had happened to her in the last few days scrolled in pictures across her mind. Bambo drinking. Spilling tea on the brown envelope. Bambo beating her. Hiding behind the grain mill. Bambo staggering after her down the road. She closed her eyes tight as she remembered the sounds of Bambo beating Mai. Fear! Terrible fear! The long ride in the ox cart. Nurses putting Mai on the trolley. Hospital corridors with their stinging antiseptic odor. Mai's bruised body lying in a high hospital bed. *Mai may die!*

Like an echo, she heard a gruff voice say, "She may die!" Kondi jumped up and peeked around the corner. Uncle Kakama, her mother's brother, and another relative stood with their backs to her outside the bus shelter. "Chisale has beaten her badly this time," Uncle Kakama said. "So badly, we don't know if she will live. She gave birth to a tiny baby boy a few minutes ago, but we don't know if he will live either."

A baby brother? But I wanted a baby sister! And Mai may die! Who will take care of me then?

"Well, if she dies, you'll have Kondi to help you," the relative said.

Kondi's eyes widened in alarm. Her breath stopped

for a minute and then she drew in a long breath.

"Big as she is, she should be able to hoe in the garden," the relative went on. "She would be another pair of strong arms for working around the house and in the garden, but she's not a very happy child."

"Kondi will not eat my food for very long. With seven children of my own to feed, we will give Kondi in marriage as a second or third wife as soon as possible. We'll be thankful for what little bride-price we can get for her." Uncle's Kakama's short laugh rang cruel and cold.

Kondi swallowed a lump in her throat. *Wife!* She didn't wait to hear more. She slipped away among still-waiting passengers into the middle of the grove of eucalyptus trees that formed a park near the bus station. She flung herself to the ground between the exposed roots of a tall tree. *I wish these huge trees would break in the wind and fall on me.* She tilted her head way back and watched the thrashing treetops far overhead. *Then I could die, too!* She bowed her head. *Oh God, let me die, too!*

For a long time she dug at the ground with a twig. She squashed any ant that dared to crawl near. The wind moaned in the giant treetops but underneath, near the ground, the silence engulfed her.

"I don't want to be a wife!" she murmured to herself. "Not yet. I'm still just a girl! I'm only twelve. And I don't ever want to be a second or a third wife!"

She began digging again at the hole while she thought. *I don't understand. I thought when I gave my heart to Jesus that I wouldn't be afraid anymore. Now*

I'm more terrified than I've ever been in my life. Mai could die! Tears of frustration ran down her cheeks. *I wanted a baby sister instead of a brother, but I wouldn't want him to die, now that he's here.*

Her thoughts spun in her head. *I always try to do what I should. I go to church every Sunday. Why is God letting these bad things happen to me?*

Suddenly she jumped to her feet. "God is not good!" she said loudly. "He let this happen. Mai Mbewe lied. She said in Sunday school that Christians are happy and they don't need to be afraid. Well, I'm not happy and I'm afraid!" Her heart felt like a huge stone inside her chest. She threw a pebble at a white pigeon that had toddled near. It rocketed away unharmed, and Kondi stalked angrily back toward the bus station and the market to buy Mai's chicken.

She didn't look up. She didn't want to see anyone she knew and have to give polite greetings. She stomped past the market gateman who held out his hand to see her identification card.

"Iwe!" the gateman shouted. "You!" He waved his hand at another market worker. "Stop that girl! She didn't show her card!"

Kondi darted amongst the shoppers. She bumped into a woman with a baby on her back, but didn't even say "Pepani." Ducking low, she wriggled between several tables piled high with clothes. The gateman and the market worker couldn't find her now. Her angry heart furrowed her forehead and twisted down the corners of her mouth. She knocked over a pile of oranges and didn't care. She nearly ran into a man bent double under a huge basket of cabbages.

"Kondi."

It was her father. Kondi froze and then slowly turned around. Could this be Bambo – the same Bambo she saw every day? He looked so different. Broken. Even...scared.

Bambo just stood there with his hands hanging down. He didn't have his brown envelope and his shirt was dirty and torn. His eyes, rimmed with red, pled with her. His face sagged, crumpled like an empty sack with all the usefulness gone out of it. "Kondi, I..." His hands fumbled with his shirt buttons, and he smoothed its wrinkles over and over again.

All her anger drained away in a rush of tears. She turned and ran. *Who is he?* Tears poured down her face. She ran and ran – anywhere, just to get away from this man who was no longer the father she knew.

Later, she could not remember buying the chicken or reaching the gate. She vaguely remembered the gateman and the market worker reaching out wiry arms to grab her. Kondi darted past them, through the gate, along the wall, and around a corner.

Sometime later, Ulemu found her sobbing under a huge poinsettia bush near the hospital, the chicken, with its feet tied, lying beside her. "Kondi." She took Kondi's arm, but Kondi didn't look up. She turned away. Ulemu's heart began to pound at the look on

Kondi's face. She'd never seen her cry like this before.

"Kondi!" Ulemu said again, grabbing her arm and giving it a little shake. "I saw you and your father inside the market."

Kondi jerked Ulemu's hand from her arm.

"You have to forgive him."

"Forgive him?" Suddenly rage boiled up inside of her. She could taste the bitterness of her hatred. "Forgive him for killing my mother and baby brother? Never." She spat in the dust at their feet. "I'll never speak to my father again as long as I live!"

"How did you hear that, Kondi?"

"Uncle Kakama was talking to a relative near the bus station. He said my mother and baby brother are dead! He's going to make me someone's third wife!" She jerked around to face Ulemu, anger flashing from her eyes. "Nobody is going to make me marry anybody. I'm just a girl. I don't want to marry yet! I'll run away! I'll die first!" Suddenly, Kondi's face crumpled and tears rushed down her cheeks again.

"Oh, Kondi. Don't cry! Your mother and baby brother are both alive. I don't know why your uncle said that, but they are both going to live." She folded Kondi into a big hug and helped her to a seat in the sun.

"They're alive?" Kondi sobbed with relief.

"Yes." Ulemu's smile was wide and beautiful. "Yes, they are. Your mother is very badly hurt, but the doctor said she will live."

Kondi's relief turned into a small smile, even

though tears still ran down her face. She scrubbed them away with the palm of her hand and wiped her hand on her skirt. The sudden change from grief to anger and then to joy made her dizzy.

Suddenly, Kondi's joy dissolved into anger and the smile on her face crumpled into ridges and planes of hatred.

"But I will never forgive my father for what he did." Kondi glared at Ulemu. "Never!"

CHAPTER 7

For the next week, Kondi stayed at the hospital with her mother. *I feel as old as those purple mountains,* she thought. Her heavy heart didn't lift, even when she sat under the three stripped peach trees and drew small pictures and designs in the dust with a twig.

Every evening she sat wrapped in her blanket on a grass mat near Mai's bed holding her baby brother. Mai liked to hear her softly sing Malawian folk songs or choruses from church. Kondi's mouth sang for Mai, but there was no song in her heart. Inside, she felt heavy like she was sick.

During the day, she cooked food, washed clothes, went to the market, and took care of her baby brother while Mai slept.

One day, Ulemu came to visit. She found Kondi sitting in the sun outside the hospital. "Moni'thu, Kondi. How are you?"

"I am well." Kondi folded a diaper and put it away in its basket. "And Mai is stronger. The doctor says she will be able to go home soon. I was afraid she would die, but God has answered the prayers you and your mother prayed for her."

"Didn't you pray, too?"

"Yes, but I don't think God would hear someone as bad as me – just you and Mai Mbewe. But I'm thankful for His goodness to my mother."

"Then why are you still sad when God has been good to you?"

"Bambo..." The words stuck in Kondi's throat, and she couldn't finish. After a bit she went on. "When I saw him in the market, he didn't seem like anybody I even knew. God doesn't always make us happy, like your mother said in Sunday school class. Why did she tell us a lie?"

"She didn't. I'm a Christian and I'm afraid and sad sometimes," Ulemu said, "but even when I'm unhappy, it's different. I'm not terrified when I'm in trouble. I think it is God who comforts me. Even if I knew I was going to die, I'd know I'd soon be with my loving heavenly Father. My mother says knowing God is what makes Christians happy, even when things are hard." Ulemu smiled. "There won't be any crying in heaven, no sickness nor death. Heaven will be a beautiful place of peace. Even when life isn't good, we can be happy remembering that."

"It sounds very nice," Kondi said with a wistful smile, "but I don't think I'm going to Heaven."

"Why, Kondi?"

"I can't forgive Bambo for what he did to my mother. Mai and Baby Brother could have died!

Bambo used to love us but I don't think he does any more." She picked up a twig, poked at a small beetle that crawled nearby and swallowed at the lump of misery in her throat. "If Bambo can't love me, how can God love me?"

"Of course your father loves you," Ulemu said. "If he'd trust God with his life, he wouldn't be so angry and mean. God can help you love your father, even when he acts ugly."

Kondi shook her head, blinking back tears. She broke the twig into tiny pieces, dropping them in her lap. She knew what Ulemu said was right.

"God's loves us, no matter what we do. Our going to heaven doesn't depend on whether people love us, only on whether we have asked Jesus to take away our sins. Have you done that?"

Kondi nodded again and wiped a tear away with the corner of her chirundu.

"Then, of course, you will be able to go to heaven when your time comes. The Bible says that God doesn't ignore us because we've done something bad. He always loves us, even when we are sinners, even really bad sinners! You know that, don't you?"

Kondi looked out over the deep valley, wiped her face again, and turned to Ulemu.

"Yes. But I don't feel forgiveness for Bambo in my heart. How can I forgive him when I don't feel like forgiving?"

"Mai says that forgiveness is a decision. The feeling sometimes comes afterward."

Kondi sniffed and wiped her cheek again. She

smiled at her friend. "I'll think about that."

Ulemu stood up, shook out her skirt, and brushed off bits of dried grass. "I'll come again tomorrow. Can I bring you anything from home?"

Kondi thought for a minute. "Yes, bring me the white baby shirt on Mai's sewing machine and my sewing basket. I want to sew something for Baby Brother." She stood up, too. "Wait. I'll tell Mai, and then I'll walk with you as far as the market."

A few minutes later, as they walked toward town, Ulemu said, "Do you know what Boniko has done now? She put a blind snake in our teacher's desk at school. Teacher fell down like she was dead when she opened her drawer. We were all terrified. Boniko was the only one who laughed, so we're sure she did it."

"I'm sorry for Teacher," Kondi said. "I suppose, even if Boniko didn't put the snake in there, that she would get the blame, because she is mean so often."

"Are you defending her?"

Kondi shook her head. "No, of course not."

When they reached the market, Kondi said, "I'll look for you tomorrow. Don't forget to bring the sewing things. If you can find Bambo's blue shirt, you can bring that, too."

"Why bring your father's blue shirt?" Ulemu asked.

"You'll have to wait and see." Kondi smiled.

After waving good-bye, she walked into the park of eucalyptus trees on the other side of the road. She sat down on a stone at the base of a tree to think. One of the street sweepers, with his besom, had swept the fallen leaves into small piles. With a flaming torch of grass, he walked from pile to pile setting each heap to smoldering. Feathers of smoke trailed into the air. The towering tree trunks let in slants of early afternoon light, like windows in a huge church. The twists of smoke, pungently fragrant, climbed the air columns between the tree arches. *Like spicy perfume, but not as sweet.* She brushed a fly away from her face. *It's quiet here—like in a church.* The hoot of a bus preparing to leave seemed far away. She sat very still.

Kondi folded her hands, but turned her back to the bus station so no one would see her. "I'm sorry, God. Please forgive me for being angry with Bambo and with You. Help me to love Bambo like You do, even when he's mean." A breeze sighed in the tree tops. She imagined her prayers rising up and up to God. "I decide to forgive Bambo now. And please help Bambo to love You—and me, too."

Back at the hospital, Kondi smiled from deep inside. Her heart felt light again. "Would you like to sit outside in the sun for a while, Mai?" she asked.

"Yes," Mai replied, "but I'm too weak to carry the baby."

"I'll carry him, if you can walk to the door." Kondi took a mkeka for Mai to sit on and picked up Baby Brother in his bundle of blankets. She walked quickly down the corridor, while Mai came slowly behind, using the wall for support. After turning the corner in the corridor, Kondi looked up. Her heart squeezed hard. Bambo stood halfway down the hall. She swallowed and held Baby Brother tighter. Her heart began to pound. *You've forgiven Bambo, Kondi. Don't forget that.*

"I've come to see your mother," he said. His eyes were not red today. His hand was steady as it smoothed the front of his shirt.

Kondi swallowed again. "Bambo," she said, but she didn't move. She cleared her throat. "Here is our new baby. Would you like to carry him?"

Bambo came close. His finger, about the same size as Baby Brother's arm, pulled the blankets away from the baby's face. Bambo's eyes softened, but he didn't smile and he didn't take Baby Brother.

"Mai is coming out to sit in the sun." Kondi pointed back down the hall to Mai coming slowly along. Bambo walked to Mai. She heard him whisper something. Mai smiled wearily. Kondi walked backward toward the sunshine-framed doorway to be sure Mai would be all right. Then she turned and went outside.

When Mai was seated on the mkeka in the hospital yard, Bambo squatted nearby. Kondi gave Baby Brother to Mai, then knelt on one knee and extended both hands to her father in the traditional greeting. "Hello, Bambo," she said, hoping her voice would not shake. "I'm glad you came to see us. I bought you a small present the other day, but I haven't had a chance to give it to you yet." She loosened her chirundu, reached into the pocket of her petticoat where she kept her treasures, and brought out the wrapped candy. It now seemed like a month ago when she'd bought it near the market gate. She gave it to Bambo with both hands, to show respect.

Bambo looked from the sweet in his hand to Kondi and back again. His eyes were soft and dark.

Can that be a tear in the corner of his eye?

"Jesus loves you, and so do I," Kondi said. "I'm sorry I was rude to you at the market."

Bambo didn't say anything; he just nodded his head. His mouth twisted, he swallowed hard, and brushed one cheek with the back of his hand. When he glanced up, a wan smile lifted one corner of his mouth. He put out his calloused hand and gently rubbed her head. "I'm sorry, too," he said. "For everything."

CHAPTER 8

Things were not the same in the hospital as they were at home. Kondi still had some of the same duties. She cooked their food in the kitchen area. After they'd eaten and she'd washed the dishes she put their food supplies and utensils neatly under Mai's bed. And there was laundry to do in the big cement basin at the back of the hospital. She spread the diapers and clothes on the grass to dry in the hot sun, but sat nearby to be sure their garments weren't blown away in a stiff wind—or stolen.

After that, there wasn't much to do; no eggs to collect from the chicken house, no yard to sweep, no water to carry from the well at the bottom of the hill, no trips to the chigayo. Ulemu and Mai Mbewe always brought firewood for cooking their meals, so she didn't even have to collect that. When she went to the market for vegetables, a chicken or dried fish, she always went in the morning before Mai became too tired to take care of Baby Brother. Sometimes, when Bambo made his daily visit, he'd bring a pound of beef or goat meat that he'd bought from a roadside butcher on the way.

Although she had a lot of time on her hands, she wasn't free to do what she wanted to do. Mai still needed her help, and she needed to stay nearby.

As Kondi sat by Mai's bed, she smiled as she thought about what to sew on Bambo's blue shirt. "I want it to be nice. What design would Bambo like?" She scratched on the ground with a twig. "No, not flowers for a man." She brushed out that design. "Men want man-things, like boats and fishing!" Soon a canoe appeared on the ground with several fish of different kinds floating under the water. "I don't know if there are real fish like these," she giggled, "but maybe they will make Bambo smile."

"What are you whispering and laughing at, Kondi?" Mai asked from her nearby mat in the sun.

Kondi quickly scratched out the picture, but it was printed on her mind. "It's a surprise," she said. "I'll show it to you when it is finished."

"All right." Mai smiled and wrapped her baby more comfortably in his blankets and handed him to her daughter. "I'm sure it will be nice." She smiled weakly, lay down on the mat and pulled a blanket over herself.

Maybe now I can tell Bambo and Mai about my drawings and embroidery. Kondi cradled Baby Brother on her arm. *I think they will like it.*

Ulemu brought the sewing things the next day, and the baby's and Bambo's shirts. "Your father seems to be sad all the time, these days," she said.

"My father has been talking to him this week and invited him to come to church, but he didn't come."

Kondi looked at the ground and sadly shook her head.

"Bambo Chisale was planting a poinsettia bush near your house and my father heard when Boniko's father laughed at him." Ulemu watched a hawk circle in the updrafts that swooped up from the deep Rift Valley. "When Boniko's father started on down the road, my father told him he thought it would look nice there by the corner of the house."

"Boniko's father made fun of him once before, and he threw the flowers away," Kondi said. "Please thank Bambo Mbewe for encouraging my father."

That afternoon, while Mai and Baby Brother slept, Kondi took a pencil stub she had found on the ground and lightly drew the boat design on the back yoke of Bambo's shirt. She also drew one of the fish on the breast pocket of Baby Brother's shirt.

"What are you doing with Bambo's shirt?" Mai asked when she woke up.

But Kondi wouldn't tell. "I hope you and Bambo will like it when it is done," was all she would say. She smiled as she quickly folded the shirt away.

Every afternoon, while Mai slept, Kondi worked on the shirts. Soon the colors began to appear behind her needle; brown for the canoe, blue for the lake, and red for the fisherman's shirt. When Mai woke up, Kondi would tuck Bambo's and Baby Brother's shirts into hiding until the next afternoon.

Mai grew stronger every day, and Baby Brother's

cheeks began to be fat and round. "We will name him Chiyembekezo. Hope," Mai said, "because there is hope in Jesus."

"That's a nice name, but I think I'll call him Kezo for short," Kondi giggled. "Chiyembekezo is an awfully long name for such a tiny boy." She tickled his cheek with her finger.

"That's true." Mai smiled. "But I want to call him Chiyembekezo because I still have hope that Bambo will ask Jesus to be his Saviour. Even though Bambo...has problems," Mai said hesitantly, wanting to be kind, "I will continue to trust in Him that Bambo will make things right with God."

Kondi swallowed at the big lump in her throat and blinked away the tears that came to her eyes. "I will, too," she said. "And Kezo will help us remember to hope."

"I can go home tomorrow," Mai said two days later after the doctor had been to see her. Ulemu and her mother had come to visit them.

"Eee! You'll be glad to go home." Ulemu said. "I will go tell your father as soon as we get home. It will be nice to have you all home again."

The next morning Kondi carefully packed all their clothes. She buttoned Bambo's blue shirt and folded it carefully, admiring the lovely fishing scene she had finished embroidering the night before. "I think he'll like it," she whispered as she slipped it into the basket with Kezo's tiny white one. "These are the very nicest designs I've ever done."

"Stop whispering to yourself, Kondi, and finish packing," Mai said a little crossly. "We don't want to keep Bambo waiting for us." Mai was still very weak, and Kondi knew anybody can be cross when they feel weak, so she stopped whispering and hurried the packing along. *I know Bambo will be happy when he sees his shirt.*

That night Kondi yawned sleepily when she rolled out her mat, lay down, and wrapped herself in her blanket. Bambo had come with an ox cart in which they bumped and jolted the eight miles home. They stopped to buy a bag of maize. When they arrived home it was time to start cooking supper, and Mai needed a nap. Kondi had cooked, served the food and tea, and then washed the dishes.

Kondi's hand clapped to her mouth and she sat straight up on her mat. "I forgot to show Bambo the shirt! I meant to do that first thing when we got home, but there was so much to do, I forgot. I'll just hang it over the back of the chair by the table where he'll see it first thing in the morning." She smiled as she heard Bambo snore in the dark. "A surprise is even better."

She wearily threw back the blanket, rummaged in her basket for the shirt, and hung it over the back of the chair. Standing on one foot in the moonlight, she brushed the shirt so the fishing design was neat and smooth. She laid Kezo's tiny shirt on the table with the fish on the pocket shining out in the moonlight. Then she went back to her mat and pulled the blanket over her head to keep the mosquitoes from biting her.

She woke with a start at the sound of a terrible crash. Thin morning light crept in the window and under the door. A chair fell over and knocked into the water bucket. *Mai-o! Mai-o!* She scrambled from under the blanket. *What is happening? Is Bambo drunk again? He was asleep when I went to bed!*

"Who did this to my shirt?" Bambo shouted. His fist crashed down onto the table. "My shirt! My best shirt is ruined!"

"Mai-o! I thought he would like it!" Kondi whispered, huddling in the corner. "Dear God, please help me now!"

CHAPTER 9

"I did, Bambo." Kondi's voice sounded small in the deep silence as Bambo stopped banging things to listen. "I embroidered your shirt, but I didn't mean to ruin it. I thought you would like it."

With a roar of anger, Bambo stormed over to Kondi's mat, his arms out to grab her. Suddenly, Mai stood between them, holding Kezo to protect his head from the blow she expected. "No, Bambo, no!" she shouted. "Leave her alone." Kezo began to wail.

Bambo stopped short, but he didn't stop shouting. "She's ruined it! My best shirt! My only good one! She's ruined it with pictures and colors." His naked shoulders glistened in the early morning light. He grabbed his red and black checked shirt and opened the door. He turned and shook a finger at Kondi. "You'll be sorry for this!" He slammed the door behind him so hard that the wall shook. Glass from the window at the top of the door tinkled down into the sudden silence. Stillness hung in the chilly morning air, broken only by the sound of Bambo's feet stomping across the yard toward the road.

"Oh, Mai, he's *very* angry! He's so angry he even forgot to take his envelope!" Kondi pointed to the ragged edge of the mysterious envelope that hung over the top of the chest of drawers standing in the corner. "I thought he would *like* a design on his shirt. Mai-o! Mai-o!"

Mai hugged Kondi with one arm and Kezo with the other. "I won't let him hurt you," Mai said rubbing Kondi's head and wiping her tears with a corner of Kezo's blanket with a shaking hand. She patted Kezo's back. "I won't let him hurt either of you."

After a while, Kondi crept to the door, stepping around the broken glass and peeked outside to see if Bambo was in sight. Then she wrapped a chirundu around her shoulders and went out to the side of the house where the morning sun shone. She turned her face to the wall to get the sun on her shivering back, and stood there for a long time soaking up warmth.

"Morning, Kondi!" Ulemu called, as she stepped out of her house across the clearing. When Kondi only gave a tiny wave of her fingers and didn't even smile, Ulemu came right over. "What's wrong?"

"Bambo's going to beat me when he comes home." Kondi told Ulemu the whole story.

"We heard shouting," Ulemu said. "What was he angry about?"

"He said I ruined his shirt, drawing pictures on it, and sewing colors." Kondi shivered even though she stood in the full sun. "I just wanted to do something nice to show I love him." She sighed deeply.

"Didn't you ask God to show you something nice to do for your father?" Ulemu asked. Kondi nodded.

"And didn't God show you to do that design on his shirt?"

"I think so." Kondi sighed again. "When things are bad, it's hard to know if it was God or if it wasn't."

"It will turn out all right." Ulemu patted Kondi's arm. "You'll see."

All day Kondi worked listlessly. She swept up the broken glass from the door, washed dishes and a few baby clothes for Kezo. In the afternoon she pounded corn, but the pestle felt almost too heavy to lift and drop, lift and drop.

"Come, Kondi," Mai said. "I need you to go to the small market. Today is butchering day, and I think it would be good to have some goat meat for supper, don't you?"

Kondi nodded her head, but she didn't look up, and she couldn't smile.

"Buy some onions, too," Mai said as she handed a few Kwacha to Kondi. "Goat meat tastes much better when onions are cooked with it."

On her way to the roadside market, a short walk from home, she stopped in the deep shade of a tree across the road from the local bar. Through the door, in the dim light inside, a red-and-black-checked arm lifted a cup to drink again and again. She hung her head, flicked a stone with her bare toe, and walked on.

"He's drinking again," she told Mai in a flat voice

when she arrived home with the meat. Later she saw Mai slip away in the direction of the bar. Kondi ran after her. "Don't, Mai. Please. You're still weak. He might hit you if you try to bring him home."

Mai stopped and turned to Kondi, then looked down at Kezo, snuggled warmly in his blanket on her arm. She nodded her head and turned back toward home.

In the middle of the night Kondi heard something fall against the door. Her eyes flew open. With one finger she slowly made a peephole in the folds of the blanket over her head. A man's head showed at the hole in the door where the small glass window had been. An arm came through the gap and turned the doorknob from the inside. Kondi's heart pounded so hard she was sure the man could hear. The door handle turned. A scream started up deep in her throat. Under her blanket Kondi clamped an icy hand over her mouth. Bambo stepped carefully through the door and closed it behind him.

He meant to be quiet, but he began to mutter to himself. "...shirt. Ruined...envelope here somewhere. Quiet..." He turned carefully around and walked into a chair, knocking it over with a crash. "Shh!" he mumbled to himself. "Quiet..." He went to the dresser and felt around for the envelope, knocking over a glass of water that Mai had put there for a night-time sip. The patter of water dripping to the floor sounded loud in the darkness. When he found it he shook the water off of it, dried it on his shirt front, and placed it carefully in the center of the table. Then he went to the bed, dropped his shoes on the floor with a clunk, and climbed in. He soon began to snore.

Kondi lay awake for a long time, watching the shadows of tree branches creep across the floor in the square of white moonlight. *At least he didn't beat me tonight, but I may get it in the morning.*

However, in the morning, Bambo was gone. The embroidered blue shirt was no longer hanging from the chair. Kondi didn't see it again for many days.

CHAPTER 10

"Hello, Kondi!"

Kondi turned her head and sighed. She recognized that saucy voice as Boniko's.

"You look very tired this morning. Did you have a bad night?"

The words are right, but it sounds as if she's making fun of me. Kondi tightened her chirundu around her waist as she turned. "Yes, I did have a bad night. Don't make fun! Mai is very tired this morning, too, and I'm worried about her." She scowled at Boniko.

"What's wrong?" Boniko looked a bit embarrassed.

Why did I tell Boniko everything, she wondered, later in the day. *It just all spilled out – Bambo's drinking, the beatings, and trying to please him by embroidering his shirt.* "I try to make him love me, but nothing seems to work," she had said with a sniff. She wiped quickly at the tears brimming in her eyes.

"Mmm." Boniko nodded solemnly. "I know a way to make your father love you."

"You do?"

"Sure. Just go to Mai Malenga. She can make things happen, you know." Boniko glanced at Kondi out of the corners of her eyes with a knowing smile.

"What do you mean by 'make things happen'?"

"You know. People call it witchcraft, but it is just a bundle of twigs that you put under their bed, or something. There's no real harm in it."

"Well, I gave my life to God," Kondi said, "so I don't want to have anything to do with witchcraft." As she walked away, Boniko chuckled softly.

Practice for the Christmas play started that week at church. They had already chosen the actors for the drama parts when Kondi was at the hospital with her mother, but she joined the choir, and they practiced every afternoon.

She took the short-cut through the back of Boniko's yard when she walked to practice. The choir sang several times during the drama, so the actors and the choir practiced together.

"Are things any better at home?" Boniko asked the first day Kondi walked through her yard to go to choir practice.

Kondi shook her head and kept looking at the ground.

"Remember, I know where you can get help"

Kondi shook her head again and walked on.

After that, it seemed as if Boniko waited for her every day. Sometimes she would just laugh softly when Kondi walked by. At other times she repeated her offer to take Kondi to Mai Malenga.

"Just leave me alone, Boniko! Bambo hasn't even come home, yet!"

"Hasn't come home?"

"No, he's been gone several days now. We don't know where he is."

"Mai Malenga could tell you where to find him – and make him love you when he comes home."

Kondi stared at Boniko thoughtfully, then turned and went on her way.

She intended to take the longer way around by the road, but every afternoon she found herself walking through the back of Boniko's yard again. Once, she stopped to talk for a while. Two days later she stayed so long that she nearly missed the play practice altogether.

By the end of the second week, Kondi sat down to help Boniko pick over a pan of beans. Before she left, she said, "Well, if it is only sticks and leaves and stuff, I guess it won't hurt to give it a try."

"You'll have to bring money," Boniko said.

Kondi looked up. "Money? I don't have any money."

"Well, you'll have to have money, or she won't give you the bundle." Boniko said it as though she was really sad. "Don't you know where you can get some money?"

Kondi remembered Mai had put ten kwacha away, to hide it from Bambo. "He'd never think to look in the kitchen rafters," she had heard Mai whisper to herself.

She glanced sideways at Boniko. "If I can find some

money, when will you take me?" An ugly feeling squeezed her stomach and made it sour. *But I have to do something so we can find Bambo and he'll love me again, don't I?* She pushed the uneasy feeling out of her mind.

Boniko grinned. "Listen, I'll take you tomorrow night. If you find the money, meet me here under this mango tree at ten o'clock." Just then Boniko's mother stepped out of their kitchen house and called to her. "Ten o'clock," Boniko whispered as she walked away.

That night at play practice everything went wrong for Kondi. Once she started singing a different song than everyone else and the whole choir began laughing. Another time she sang right out when one of the drama players was supposed to speak.

"What's wrong, Kondi?" Ulemu whispered.

Kondi just shook her head and covered her face with her hands. When practice was over, Kondi edged toward the back door and slipped out alone while Ulemu was chatting. She didn't want to walk home with anyone tonight.

When she arrived home, Bambo sat at the table eating his supper with Mai, holding Kezo, sitting nearby. Bambo didn't say a word to her, but his blue shirt wasn't with him.

The next evening Kondi pretended she was tired

and rolled up in her blanket early. Bambo, Mai and Kezo went to bed in the next room around nine o'clock. Kondi lay as still as she could. She could hear a cricket crick-crick-cricking at the corner of the house. Frogs croaked in the dambo at the bottom of their hill and others answered them from the ditch by the road. Kondi's heart pounded as, with a cautious hand, she pulled back the edge of the blanket to look at the luminous dial on the clock. Twenty minutes to ten.

I shouldn't do this. I'm glad Bambo is home again, but I want very much for him to love me. She pulled the blanket back over her head again. A mosquito buzzed outside the blanket.

When she thought ten minutes were up, she pulled the blanket away and sat up. Just then an owl flew across the moonlight at the window. Kondi's heart stopped and she jumped as if someone had stuck a thorn in her back. Everyone knew that an owl was a bad omen!

"Whoo?" the owl hooted.

Kondi covered her ears.

A few minutes later the door creaked when she slipped outside. She walked across the bare ground of their bwalo to the kitchen house out back. Entering, she stood on a stool under a rafter pole. *It's not really cold. Why am I shivering?* Her hands trembled as she took the money down, tied it in the corner of her chirundu and tucked the corner into her waist. *I'm not afraid. I won't be afraid.*

She found Boniko under the mango tree where

she'd promised to meet her. Kondi stumbled as they walked toward Mai Malenga's medicine house. Fear prickled across her dry tongue. She tried to lick her lips, but it felt like rubbing a stick over a dry corn cob.

Ten minutes later, a strange odor came to her nostrils as she walked in Mai Malenga's medicine house door with Boniko. Firelight glittered in Mai Malenga's eyes as she motioned for them to sit down. She said, "I have your bundle, Kondi." She held up a small packet for Kondi to see. "Do you have the money?"

Kondi swallowed hard and nodded her head.

"Give it to me."

Kondi didn't move. *I won't be afraid! If it is only sticks and leaves, I shouldn't be afraid of that!* But her heart went on bumping hard against her ribs, and she licked her lips as she gulped down the panic in her throat. She lifted a shaking hand and wiped at the sweat on her forehead.

"Kondi, give me the money!"

Perfect love casts out fear! The memory verse that Kondi had learned in Sunday school rang loudly in her ears. *That's why I'm afraid. If I really loved God, I wouldn't be doing this.*

"The money, Kondi!" A dark frown creased Mai Malenga's forehead. She dangled the packet in front of Kondi's eyes and swung it back and forth, back and forth. "Give me the money."

"No!" Kondi scrambled to her feet. Her heart pounded in her ears, and icy tingles ran down her arms into her fingertips.

"Eh?"

"No. I've changed my mind. I don't want it!" Kondi's voice was loud in the fire-flickering stillness. "Jesus doesn't like what I'm doing. I'm leaving." Kondi's heart pounded like a drum in the night. Could Boniko hear it? Twisting sideways to get away from Mai Malenga's reaching hands, Kondi slid along the wall. Boniko's mocking laugh followed her as she slipped through the open doorway and ran into the moonlit darkness toward home.

Ragged clouds tore across a huge white moon making black shadows run along the ground. Poinsettia bushes, taller than her head, rustled and thrashed in a cold wind and the giant eucalyptus trees twisted and bent. Kondi stopped to catch her breath in the shadow of a hibiscus bush. Glancing behind her, she saw Mai Malenga running toward her across the yard. Kondi turned and ran like a hare, darting from bush to bush. Branches plucked at her clothing and leaves whipped her face as she ran. She could hear Mai Malenga's feet slapping on the hard ground behind her.

Kondi stumbled over a rock. She threw out her hands to catch herself, grabbed the rough bark of a tree trunk and ran on. Her fingers burned. Something large and black crashed away through the brush near her. Blood smeared her mouth when she put up her hand to stifle a scream. Fear peaked when, glancing behind her, she saw Mai Malenga close on her heels. She jumped behind a bush, twisted away from the path, and dashed on. Her foot caught on an exposed root she hadn't seen in the half-light and she fell hard, hitting her head against a boulder. She lay very still.

Mai Malenga's dark figure approached and stood over Kondi's still body, arms akimbo. The old woman chuckled wickedly, checked her hands to find the money. The little wretch didn't bring any money after all. She spat on the ground near Kondi's head and turned away.

Ten minutes later Kondi sat up. She touched her head where a big lump swelled and throbbed. She shivered. A fine rain had sprung up on the cold wind while she lay unconscious on the ground. *How long have I been lying here?* She pulled her soaking dress away from her body. *I want to go home!* Standing shakily to her feet, her eyes darted into every shadow as she stumbled on toward home.

When she reached their kitchen house she dashed inside and hid in a corner. No one had followed. The goats in their paddock stirred and bleated mournfully in the rain. She held one hand to her head and the other over her heart to still its drumming and catch her breath. *Did I just imagine that someone followed me? My knees are weak.* Shakily she turned over a bucket to stand on, braced her hand on the wall, and put the ten kwacha back on the rafter.

Tiptoeing to their house she carefully turned the door handle. It groaned loudly in the dark.

"Ahh!" Bambo shouted, waking up. "Who's coming

into my house?" He scrabbled with his blankets. Kondi ran into a corner and covered her head with her arms. Bambo's feet thudded to the floor in the next room.

She raised her head. "It's just me, Bambo." She hoped her voice didn't shake as badly as her body trembled.

After a moment of dead silence the bed creaked as Bambo swung his legs back into bed. "Mm-hm," he mumbled. "Next time, be quiet when you come in from the outhouse?"

Kondi hardly breathed. After a few minutes she took off her soaking dress and crawled under her blanket. She listened until she heard Bambo's even breathing. He was asleep.

CHAPTER 11

"I don't want you to pound maize with me this morning. You'll have a headache." Mai touched Kondi's shoulder gently. "How did you bump your head last night? You have a lump as big as an egg."

"I was half asleep and walked into a tree," Kondi lied. She knew it was wrong to tell an untruth. *But I had to, this time. I couldn't tell her what I did.*

Her shame about last night made her insist on helping her mother even though her head throbbed to the steady beat of their pounding pestles, crushing the maize kernels in the same big wooden mortar, one heavy pestle going up as the other came down. Kezo, contentedly asleep, bounced rhythmically on Mai's back as the long poles alternately rose and fell. Kondi softly sang a pounding song; not really a song, more like her thoughts expressed in a sing-song voice to the rhythm of the pestle's beat.

"Kondi, will you go in the house and get a chirundu for me?" Mai asked. "Now that the sun is on us, my head is getting hot. I'll use the chirundu for a head wrap to keep me cool."

Kondi's song died away as the rhythm of the pounding broke. "Yes, Mai." She put the pestle carefully on the ground and rubbed her forehead to ease its aching. A scarf tied tightly around her head would ease the pain, but the sore lump in her hair made that impossible.

It was dark and cool inside as she opened the door a crack and slipped through. *Mai probably thought I was coming in from the outhouse last night, too. She would be ashamed to call me her daughter if she knew where I'd really been.* Her heart started to race as she remembered her wild, lonely dash through the night.

Mai's chirundu lay over the back of a chair in the sitting room. Kondi started to reach for it. Out of the corner of her eye she saw something fall through the bedroom door. A draft from the open door fluttered some papers to the floor from the dresser top.

I'd better pick those up. She stepped through the doorway and stooped, reaching out to pick up the first sheet. *Mai-o!* She jerked her hand back and dropped to one knee in dismay. *Bambo's mysterious envelope! Mai-o! Now what should I do?* Several sheets of paper and Bambo's tattered envelope lay scattered on the floor. *Should I pick them up or leave them?* Kondi's hand went to her mouth.

"If I leave them," she whispered to herself, "he'll be cross that I was careless, but if he comes in and finds me with them in my hand, I'll get another beating!"

Thoughts raced through her mind as she puzzled over the situation. "Why would Bambo leave his envelope? He always takes it with him when he goes out," she muttered to herself. "I haven't seen him for over an hour. Maybe he just forgot. I'll pick them up and put them back in the envelope, but I won't look at them at all!"

When Kondi picked up the first paper she caught a glimpse of colors. She couldn't resist taking one peek. "Oh!" She took a full look at the paper. "Oh!"

The door opened wider behind her. Kondi was so captured by the colors on the paper that she didn't hear the footstep on the threshold. A dark shadow slipped through the door and hovered behind her. Bambo! An angry scowl of menace crossed his face. He grasped a chair by the table and slowly, silently raised it over his head. Still, Kondi saw only the paper trembling in her hand. Bambo's muscles bulged as he lifted the chair to bring it crashing over her back.

"Oh, it is beautiful!" Her breath came out in a long sigh.

"Eh?" Bambo jerked the chair to a stop in mid-air. "What did you say?"

Kondi twisted around and threw up her arm to protect her head. Trembling, she scooted as far away from him as she could and peered at Bambo under her arm, waiting for the chair to crash over her head.

Bambo, stiff with shock, held the chair over his head for a long minute that seemed more like an hour. "What did you say?" Bambo set the chair on the floor and shakily sat down on it.

"I said it is beautiful." Kondi lowered the arm she

had flung up to protect her head. Suddenly she forgot that Bambo had been about to hit her. "Oh, Bambo! Why didn't you tell me you could draw beautiful pictures like this? Look at the colors!"

Bambo turned his face away, and began to smooth the front of his shirt as if to soothe away some trouble. "It is not beautiful. The animal is too big and the colors are not right." His voice was gruff with disappointment.

"The animal is all right," Kondi said, pointing to the drawing. "Its back leg is too big, that's all. And the colors are wonderful, but they are just too bright to be real."

"Mmm." Bambo's comment was a low rumble in his throat.

Kondi thought he was about to be angry again and jumped to her feet, ready to dart out the door, but Bambo wasn't even looking at her. He was looking at the drawing Kondi handed him.

"You are right. The back leg would look better if I made it smaller, and I can rub out some of the color with a soft eraser." He opened the top dresser drawer and took out a slender box. When he opened it, she saw brightly colored pencils and a pen. Bambo took out an eraser and went to the table. He didn't even look at her again.

Quietly Kondi took Mai's chirundu from the chair back and crept out the door.

"What's the matter, Kondi? You're trembling. Are you all right?" Mai asked as she took the chirundu.

"Yes, I'm all right," Kondi said, but her thoughts

were not on pounding maize. She stared at the ground, and then she sat down suddenly on a low stool and looked out over the valley. She put her chin in her hands and propped her elbows on her knees. The mountains had lost their purple in the noonday sun and the greenish-brown patchwork of the valley cornfields shimmered in a haze of heat. But, all she could see was the look of bright interest on Bambo's face as he began to work on his drawing.

"Kondi...?" Mai looked troubled.

"It is all right, Mai. Bambo is in the house. I'll tell you about it after we spread the cracked corn in the sun to dry," Kondi said. A faint smile hovered around her lips, but her dark brown eyes twinkled with pleasure.

Later, while Mai nursed Kezo under the shady eaves of the house, Kondi spread the last of the cracked maize on a mat laid out in the sun. Bambo called her from the shadowed doorway.

"Come out into the sunshine, Bambo, where we can see your work, your drawing." Kondi smiled at the surprise waiting for Mai.

Mai's head jerked up. Kondi could almost read her mother's mind. *Work? Bambo hasn't worked for several months. What does my daughter mean?*

Bambo hesitated in the shadow, so Kondi took his arm and led him to his favorite place in the yard.

They sat down together and began to pore over the piece of paper in Bambo's hand.

"Much better!" Kondi said with a smile.

Bambo shyly smiled back.

"Now, if you draw this edge of the leg like this..." Kondi pointed.

Puzzled, Mai got up and looked over their shoulders. When Mai's shadow fell on the paper Bambo pulled it to his chest frowning.

"Let her see it, Bambo. It's so beautiful!" Kondi's smile of delight won him over and he slowly lowered the paper to his knees.

For a minute sunlight dazzled on the paper so Mai couldn't see well. Then she saw a lovely picture of an antelope and her fawn feeding in a dambo with water glinting nearby. Flowers blew in a light breeze and a tiny bird sang from his perch on a bare tree branch.

"I saw them at our dambo...early morning a few days ago," Bambo said with an apologetic rub at his nose.

Mai's breath caught. "Of course it's our dambo. I saw that right away. What a beautiful picture."

"That's just what I said!" Kondi clapped her hands together. "This is what was in his mysterious envelope. I think there are more of them, too."

She glanced at Bambo. A slow smile started at the corners of his mouth.

"I knew it!" Kondi jumped up and began to jig in delight. Suddenly she stopped. "But why did you hide them, Bambo?" She bent over and looked deeply into her father's eyes. "Why did you hide them from those who love you?"

Bambo flicked a speck of eraser dust from his picture, turned it carefully over onto a small table, and anchored it against the breeze with a smooth clean stone. He turned his head away and began to smooth the front of his shirt again. "People who draw pictures and plant flowers in their yards are laughed at. You know that." He hung his head with embarrassment. "The men at the bar made fun of me for a week, just because I trimmed the grass eaves of our roof in an even line. The village women must think I'm a strange kind of man for a husband and father." Gentleness flooded his face as he looked at Mai holding Kezo, and then Kondi.

Why, Bambo's loved me all the time! Kondi stood and brushed the dust from her chirundu. *I can see it in his eyes. He loves me!*

"People will think I'm a stupid man, to draw pictures." Bambo turned his head away.

"Not if you earn a living that way," Kondi said.

Bambo's head spun around. "Eh?" His eyes brightened. "What did you say?"

"I said, people won't laugh if you make a living by selling your drawings." Kondi felt a smile begin to stretch from ear to ear. "They'll respect you instead."

Bambo snorted. "And how can I afford paint and canvas to get started?" He squeezed his eyes shut and turned his head away again. "I saved two tambala a week to buy those pencils!" He pointed to his picture as the result. "I don't even have a job to support you, your mother, and Kezo, much less waste what little money we have on drawing materials."

"We'll help you, Bambo!" Kondi felt too happy to be discouraged; she danced a jig around the yard. She flapped her hands at a hen pecking at the maize spread in the sun and stopped in a flurry of dust in front of her mother. "We will! We will, won't we, Mai?"

A lovely smile spread across Mai's face. "Of course we will!" She tickled Kezo's cheek making him coo, and then smiled up at Bambo. "Of course we will. We'll think of a way. Together!"

CHAPTER 12

Three weeks later, on a Sunday morning, Kondi stood by Ulemu in the choir at the front of the church.

"When you have found Him," the oily voice of King Herod was saying, "come again to me, so I, too, can go and worship Him."

The drama had started and the choir waited for their cue to sing "Joy to the World."

Kondi had heard it all so many times during drama and choir practice that her mind began to drift. *I can't believe this is my last Sunday in this church. Tomorrow we move to our new home by the highway. Moving will give Bambo a chance to earn a living by selling his drawings to tourists who drive by, but, oh, how I hate to leave all my friends!*

She looked out over the Christmas worshippers and saw so many familiar faces. In the women's section of the church, Ulemu's mother smiled at the two girls standing side by side in the choir. Mai sat next to her with Kezo snuggled in a large warm towel, then wrapped around and around in a chirundu. *Like baby Jesus is swaddling clothes.* Kondi smiled. She glanced behind her at the paper banner on the front wall of the church. *I wonder who painted it.* The banner read, JESUS, KING OF KINGS AND LORD OF LORDS!

Her face clouded when she glanced at the men's section. Her eyes searched every row of benches for Bambo. *I asked him to come and see the play, and he's not here. Maybe I've just missed him somehow.* Her eyes scanned the rows again from front to back, and then from back to front, but Bambo wasn't there. *I guess I'd be surprised if he was here, since he was out drinking again late last night.* Kondi frowned, stared at the floor, and sighed.

Ulemu poked her with a bony elbow. Kondi jumped and opened her mouth to sing out "Jo-o-y..." but caught herself before she made a sound.

"You'd better pay attention!" Ulemu whispered softly.

Kondi intended to listen, but as the drama players continued their speeches her mind drifted again. She thought back over their long discussion with Bambo. It was hard for him to see how they could start a business together as a family. Mai and Kondi had the vision and the enthusiasm, but Bambo was very practical; he wanted to be sure it would pay.

"Moving to a new home near the highway will give you more customers to buy your paintings. People who drive by will see your shop and stop to look. We could even sell roasted corn and fresh bread rolls.

Mai and I will make that," Kondi assured him.

"I don't know," Bambo murmured. "I just don't know if we can make such a move pay."

"Kondi and I will work hard to make enough for our move," Mai said. "You'll see. We can do it – together."

Mai and Kondi had worked hard during the last three weeks, Mai at her sewing machine and Kondi embroidering the clothing that Mai sewed. They surprised Bambo with how much money they made in such a short time. It was enough for them to hire an ox cart to move their few belongings, to rent a room near the piece of land where the chief said they could build their new house, and a bit left over for a few yards of cloth for more baby clothes and canvases for Bambo to work on.

It is exciting, but it is scary to move. I'll be a long way from my friends, but Ulemu will come see me when she walks in to the town market, and I can walk out here and see everybody sometimes. Kondi fidgeted, restlessly. *There will be new girls to meet in the town church where Mai and I will go on Sundays. Starting a new school won't be much fun, but I'll try to make some new friends before school starts so it won't seem so strange.*

Ulemu's elbow dug into Kondi's side again.

"Ouch!" Kondi whispered. "Stop poking me!"

Ulemu didn't even turn her head, but only made a small gesture with her chin toward the men's section. There was Bambo. Ulemu's father stood, smiled, and offered Bambo his seat.

Bambo slipped onto the last bench and Bambo Mbewe sat beside him.

"My father asked your father to make the banner for the play," Ulemu whispered, smiling.

Bambo wore the blue shirt Kondi embroidered for him. *It looks as nice as I thought it would.*

Ulemu's elbow poked Kondi's ribs again. "Joy to the World..." the choir sang. Still surprised that Bambo had come, Kondi missed the first whole phrase of the Christmas song. But she joined in on the second one. "Let earth receive her King!" Joy welled up in her heart that Bambo would hear about Jesus. "Let every heart prepare Him room! And heaven and nature sing..."

The song ended and she relaxed until their next song. *Things have been better at home since we discovered his lovely pictures. He's stayed home more, and been drinking less often. But when he knows Jesus as his Savior, we can have a really happy family. And Kezo will grow up without knowing what it is like to have Bambo beat him when he is drunk. I'm going to pray for Bambo every day, that He will accept Jesus as his Savior.*

"Oh come all ye faithful, joyful and triumphant," sang the choir. "Oh come ye, oh come ye..."

Yes, come Bambo! Kondi prayed in her heart as she sang the words. She sang with all her might! "Oh come let us adore Him, Christ the Lord!"

GLOSSARY

(Pronunciations are not given for English words)

Agogo (Ah-go'-go)
Grandparents. The plural form is often used in speaking about one person, as a term of respect.

Bambo (Bah'mbo)
Father or Mr.

Besom
A broom made of twigs for sweeping the yard.

Blind snake
A large worm that moves like a snake, but has no head.

Bwalo (Bwah'low)
Yard. It is hoed clean of grass to prevent snakes from coming near the house.

Chameleon
A slowly-creeping lizard-like creature. It hisses and it rolls its eyes around independently.

Chigayo (Chee-gah'yo)
A mill for grinding grain.

Chikondi (Chee-koh'-ndee)
Joy, happiness--often used as a girl's name.

Chiyembekezo (Chee-yem-beh-keh'-zoh)
Hope. Sometime used as a name.

Chirundu (Chee-roo'ndoo)
A piece of cloth wrapped around the waist, used for a skirt, or to carry babies on the back, or to wrap around shoulders when cold. An extra one may be taken to market to carry home flour or grain.

Dambo (Dah'-mboh)
A damp spot, usually at the base of a hill, where vegetables can be grown in the dry season.

Dedza (Deh'-dzah)
A town in Malawi. It is about 50 miles south of Lilongwe, the capital city.

Eya (Eh-yah')
Yes.

Galimoto (Gah'-lee-moh-toh)
Automobile.

Garner
A small house for storing maize.

Gourd
A squash with a hard skin. Africans dry them and hollow them out for bowls and dippers.

Gogo (Goh'-goh)
Grandmother or grandfather.

Hodi (Hoh'-dee)
A word called at someone's yard or doorway indicating they want to enter.

Hull
The outer skin of each maize kernel.

Iai (Ee-yah'-ee)
No.

Inde (Ee'-ndeh)
Yes.
Inde'di (Ee-ndeh'-dee)
Yes, indeed.
Iwe (Ee'-weh)
You. It is used to address children or as an insolent epithet to an adult.
Jacaranda (Jah-kah-rah'-nda)
A tall tree with lavender blossoms.
Kondi (Koh'-ndee)
An abbreviation of Chikondi.
Kwacha (Kwah'-chah)
Freedom. Also the name for their paper money.
Lowani (Loh-wah'-nee)
Come in.
Madzi (Mah'-dzee)
Water.
Mai (Mah'-ee)
Mother or Mrs.
Mai-o! (Mah'-ee-oh)
In moments of calamity, East and Central Africans often for their mothers.
Maize
White field corn; a Malawian's main food.
Mango (Mang'-goh)
A tree bearing delicious tropical fruit.
Mkeka (Mkeh'-kah)
A finely woven grass mat.
Moni (Moh'-nee)
Hello.

Moni-thu (Moh-nee′-too)
Hello, indeed! (usually as a reply to someone's greeting)
Mortar
A heavy container hollowed out of a log, in which Africans pound grain.
Nsima (Nsee′-mah)
A very thick porridge made of maize meal. It is the staple of a Malawian's diet.
Omen
A portent, a prophetic sign.
Pestle
The heavy pole used with the mortar to pound grain.
Pepani (Pay-pah′-nee)
Sorry.
Protea (Proh′-tee-yah)
A flowering bush of Eastern and Southern Africa.
Tambala (Tah-mbah′-lah)
Rooster. It is also the "cents" of their money system and a symbol of their freedom.
Ufa (Oo′-fah)
Maize flour.
Ulemu (Oo-leh′-moo)
Grace, courtesy. Sometimes used as a girl's name.
Zedi (Zeh′-dee)
Indeed. (Often abbreviated at the end of a word as "′di")

About the Author

Sylvia Stewart grew up in the (then) Belgian Congo. She spent 21 years as an Assemblies of God missionary in Malawi, East Africa, with her husband, Duane. While there, she taught some writing workshops, which are now bearing fruit. She started writing Kondi's Quest hoping to weave a story for the children of Malawi.

In 1992 they were asked to go to Ethiopia to found a Bible College. They spent 11 years in Ethiopia doing mostly Bible College ministry. She taught college-level English to students who had never taken a grammar class before.

Sylvia has been published in Assemblies of God denominational magazines: *The Pentecostal Evangel* (now *Today's Pentecostal Evangel*); *Advance* (now *Enrichment*); *Woman's Touch*, and their missions magazine, *Mountain Movers*, which is no longer in print. She has also been published in *WASI Writer*, a writer's magazine published under the auspices of the University of Malawi.

Sylvia is the mother of four children, who grew up in Africa. Her eleven grandchildren are the delight of her life.

Made in the USA
Coppell, TX
29 October 2021